For the Hall family

THE GREAT GRANNY ROBBERY

written and illustrated by
Rob Lewis

Macdonald

One night, something odd was happening.
All over town, people were disappearing.

The next morning, Kate and Oliver discovered
that their granny had gone.

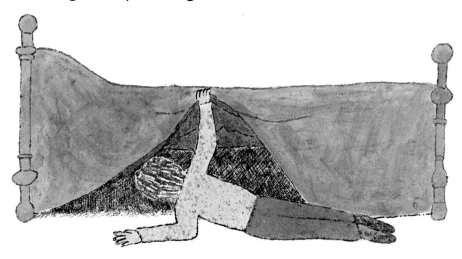

They looked all over the house but
there was no sign of her.

Then they heard the news on the television.

'Grannies all over the town have disappeared. The police are mystified.'

What nobody knew was that all the grannies
had been kidnapped by a band of evil robbers,
led by the nastiest, cruellest, wickedest
robber in the land, called Len the Laugher.
He was called Len the Laugher because
he had the nastiest, cruellest, wickedest laugh.

The robbers drove the grannies to secret factories
in the marshes. Then they forced them to knit
woolly jumpers and socks, all day long.
They planned to sell the clothes
and make lots and lots of money.

The grannies who couldn't or wouldn't knit
were turned into wax models by a machine
that Len the Laugher had invented.
Then he sold them to shops as dummies.

A few days later,
Kate, Oliver, mum and the dog were out shopping.
'Look mum! There's granny in that window,'
yelled Kate.
'This is no time for silly jokes,' said mum.
But Kate was sure.

Kate and Oliver went back to the shop
and explained to the assistant that
it was their granny in the window.
The kind shopkeeper agreed to give her back.

When they got home, they put the dummy
in front of the fire, and slowly the wax melted.
It *was* granny!

Granny did a few exercises to loosen up
her stiff arms and legs
and then she told them about
the factories in the marshes
and Len the Laugher.
They thought up a plan to free the other grannies.

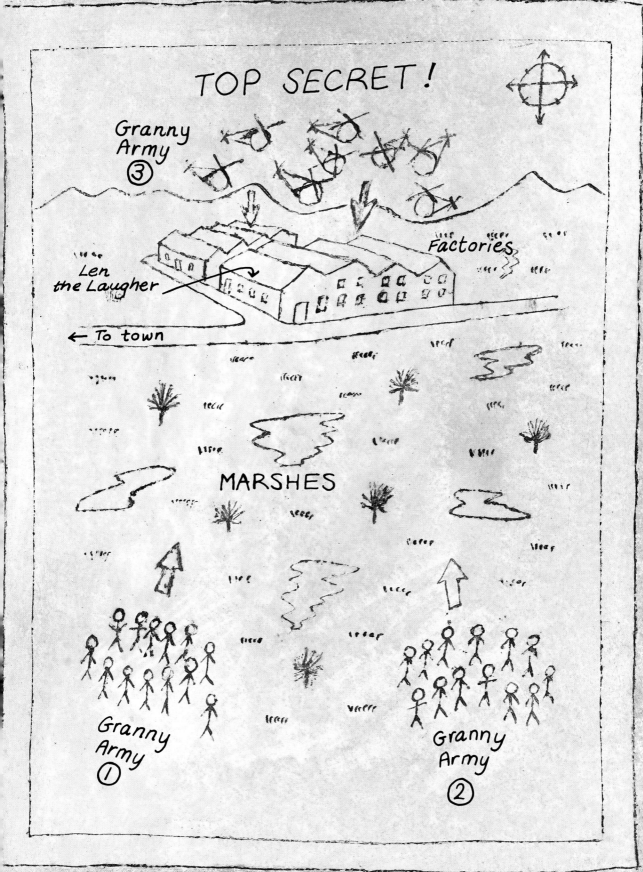

Granny rang up all the meanest, toughest, grannies
she knew. They came from far and wide
and together, they marched on the factories.

Some of them crept up through the marshes

and burst in through the doors.
and frightened the robbers so much
that they turned tail
and ran for their lives.

The rest of the grannies
flew over the factories in helicopters
and dropped a huge net on the fleeing robbers.

The battle was won!

But wait! Len the Laugher was escaping along a secret path through the marshes.

Thwak! Granny got him with her umbrella.
Kate and Oliver tied him up with knitting wool
while he was unconscious
and then they telephoned the police.

Len the Laugher isn't laughing anymore.

Other picture books by Rob Lewis published by Macdonald
Hello Mr Scarecrow
Friska the Sheep that was Too Small
The White Bicycle
Come Back Hercules

A MACDONALD BOOK

© Rob Lewis 1987

First published in Great Britain in 1987
by Macdonald & Co (Publishers) Ltd
London & Sydney
A Member of Maxwell Pergamon
Publishing Corporation plc

Reprinted 1988

Printed and bound in Spain by Cronion S.A.

Macdonald & Co (Publishers) Ltd
Greater London House
Hampstead Road
London NW1 7QX

British Library Cataloguing in Publication Data

Lewis, Rob
   The great granny robbery.
   I. Title
   823'.914 [J] PZ7
   ISBN 0–356–11847–9
   ISBN 0–356–11848–7 Pbk